This
BooK
BELONGS
To
cathy

LITTLE CRITTER'S LITTLE SISTER'S BIRTHDAY

BY
MERCER MAYER

To Geraldine & Edgar

A Golden Book • New York

Western Publishing Company, Inc., Racine, Wisconsin 53404

It was my little sister's birthday.
We were going
to give her
a party.
She did not know that.

Dad and I went shopping.
My little sister wanted
to go, too.
But she had to stay home.

We were going
to get her
birthday present.
She did not know that.

Dad and I went
to the mall.
We were going
to the toy store.

This would be a good present.
But so would this.

Or this.
This would be a good present, too.

But so would this.
Or this.

But that would be the best present. For my little sister, I mean.

We went home.
I put the present
in a box.
I got dressed.

I gave my little sister
her present.

The doorbell rang.
Surprise!
There were all of
my little sister's friends.

There were a lot of friends.
There were a lot of presents.

We went outside
to play games.
We had a bag race.

We had an egg race.

Then we went inside.
We played more games.

Mom brought out
the birthday cake.

My little sister
made a wish.
She blew out
all the candles.

Mom cut the cake.

There was a lot
of cake.

There was a piece
for everyone.

There was ice cream, too.

Then it was time
to open the presents.

My little sister
opened my present.
"Look at this!"
she cried.

She said it was
the best present.
I knew that.